Behind my Bellybutton

Elaine Tomski

Illustrated by Chris Danger

Ambassador International
GREENVILLE, SOUTH CAROLINA & BELFAST, NORTHERN IRELAND

www.ambassador-international.com

Behind My Bellybutton

Illustrated by Chris Danger
Edited by Brenda Covert

ISBN: 978-1-62020-286-9
eISBN: 978-1-62020-389-7

Page Layout: Hannah Nichols
Ebook Conversion: Anna Riebe

AMBASSADOR INTERNATIONAL
Emerald House
427 Wade Hampton Blvd
Greenville, SC 29609, USA
www.ambassador-international.com

AMBASSADOR BOOKS
The Mount
2 Woodstock Link
Belfast, BT6 8DD, Northern Ireland, UK
www.ambassadormedia.co.uk

The colophon is a trademark of Ambassador

This book is dedicated to those I hold near to my heart: my husband Jeff, my once teeny, tiny Adam and Lauren, to Ryan, Cameron, Bennett, and to God our Creator.

"That's not true!" Eli scolded his brother, jumped from the bed, and stomped down the stairs.

Finding Mama in the kitchen, Eli cried, "It's my birthday, but I'm not happy. Thomas says I'm only little."

Scooping Eli onto her lap, Mama said, "Today I'm remembering that once you were only little.

When God created you for Daddy and me, you were the size of this teeny tiny poppy seed on my muffin. That's the day God put you in a safe, warm place behind my bellybutton and near to my heart."

"What was I doing there?" asked Eli.

"You were getting bigger as fast as you could grow," said Mama.

"Now I'm big enough to eat a whole muffin!" shouted Eli.

"That's true," said Mama.

During breakfast, Eli poked at the blueberries floating in his cereal bowl. "Was I ever the size of a blueberry?" he asked.

"Once you were the size of a blueberry," Mama said.

"What was I doing then?"

"Your heart was beating strong like a drum in the safe, warm place behind my bellybutton and near to my heart."

"Now my heart beats super-duper fast when Thomas and I chase Daddy."

"That's true," said Mama.

Later that morning at the grocery store, Eli sniffed the strawberries, spied the shiniest apple, and picked up a great big orange. He asked, "Was I ever the size of an orange?"

"Once you were the size of an orange," Mama said.

"What was I doing then?"

"You were wiggling your fingers and sucking your thumb in the safe warm place behind my bellybutton and near to my heart."

"Now I can use my fingers and thumbs to put ice cream and sprinkles in the cart. Please?"

"Yes, you may," Mama said with a laugh.

That afternoon in the park, Eli and Thomas threw a softball high into the air. Mama and Buddy rested nearby. "Was I ever the size of a softball?" Eli asked Mama.

"Once you were the size of a softball," Mama said.

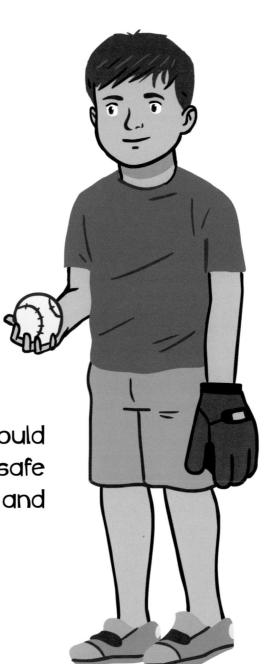

"What was I doing then?"

"You were busy listening. You could hear Buddy bark even from the safe warm place behind my bellybutton and near to my heart."

"Now I can hear lots of things like honking horns and train whistles."

"That's true," said Mama.

That evening at the picnic table, Eli spit seeds from his mouth to ask, "Was I ever the size of a watermelon?"

"Once you were the size of a watermelon," Mama said.

"What was I doing then?"

"You were super squished and trying to stand on your head behind my bellybutton."

"Was I squished for long?"

"Not for long. The day finally came when God said, 'Eli, today is your birthday!'"

Mama sat a cake with lit candles on the table for Eli. Puff! Eli blew out all of the candles with one huge breath.

Yum, yum! Eli ate cake and ice cream topped with loads of sprinkles. Then, excusing himself from the table, Eli stood on tiptoes next to Daddy.

He yelled, "Look at me now! I'm almost as tall as Daddy. God is growing me bigger every day."

"That's true," said Mama. "Do you know what else is true?"

"What, Mama?"

"No matter how many birthdays you have, no matter how big you grow, you will always be near to my heart.

Happy birthday, Eli,"
said Mama.

And it was.

You made all the delicate, inner parts of my body and knit me together in my mother's womb.

~ Psalm 139:13